This book is your book. I wrote it for you. —Love, S.L.-J.

For Elizabeth, with love —J.D.

Text copyright © 2015 by Sally Lloyd-Jones
Jacket art and interior illustrations copyright © 2015 by Jane Dyer

All rights reserved. Published in the United States by Schwartz & Wade Books,
an imprint of Random House Children's Books, a division of Random House LLC,
a Penguin Random House Company, New York.

Schwartz & Wade Books and the colophon are trademarks of Random House LLC.

Visit us on the Web! randomhouse.com/kids
Educators and librarians, for a variety of teaching tools, visit us at RHTeachersLibrarians.com

Library of Congress Cataloging-in-Publication Data
Lloyd-Jones, Sally. The house that's your home / by Sally Lloyd-Jones ;
illustrated by Jane Dyer. – First edition.
pages cm
Summary: Celebrates all the things that make one's home special,
including the family that dwells there.
ISBN 978-0-375-85884-0 (hc) – ISBN 978-0-375-95884-7 (glb) – ISBN 978-0-375-98798-4 (ebook)
[1. Home—Fiction. 2. Family life—Fiction.] I. Dyer, Jane, illustrator. II. Title. III. Title: House that is your home.
PZ7.L77878Hm 2015   [E]—dc23   2014005641

The text of this book is set in Jane Dyer's hand lettering.
The illustrations are rendered in gouache and pencil on 140-lb. cold press paper.
MANUFACTURED IN CHINA
2 4 6 8 10 9 7 5 3 1
First Edition

The House that's Your Home

by **Sally Lloyd-Jones**

illustrated by **Jane Dyer**

schwartz & wade books · new york

Mia,
I hope you like to read.
Reading will let you travel
anywhere you would like
forever ever......

Love
Judi
your Italian Aunt
march 2019

A girl is a Daughter

And a boy is a Son

And a mommy is Your Mommy

And a daddy is Your Daddy

And you are a Family

Together

In the house that's Your Home.

A cat is Your Cat

And a dog is Your Dog

And they are Your Pets.

Up the stairs is a room

With Your Name on its door

That's the room of Your Own

In the house that's Your Home

With a window to show you the sky.

A book is Your Book
And a ball is Your Ball
And they are Your Things.

And the shoes on your feet

That you use when you stomp

Are to carry you out

Of the door of the house

That's Your Home.

A field is Your Yard,

The grass where you play.

And the ground is a bed

For the seeds that you grew

Into poppies and peas

And fiddlehead ferns

For the garden of Your Own

Of the house that's Your Home.

A tree is Your Tree
That stands in Your Yard,
Your place where you go
That's holding Your Swing
And listening
Quietly
For you.

And your Swing is to swing you

Right up to the sky,

Up over the wall,

Up, up, till you see

Swallows and cornfields

And tractors and sheep

And the world that is waiting below.

Look! There is Your Garden!

Your Window!

Your Room!

There is the roof

Of the house that's Your Home!

And the stones on the ground
Are a path for Your Feet
To carry you back
To the door of the house
That's Your Home.

A grandma is Your Grandma
And a grandpa is Your Grandpa
And their legs won't go fast
And they're all full of years
But their stories are strong
And their hearts are so big
And they love you so much
That they can't ever stop.
And they belong to each other
And to you.

A bed is Your Bed
That's a ship to the moon,
To the space of the sky
That is holding the stars
And the vast Milky Way
And the dreams
That belong
Just to You.

And the moon shines down on
Your Bed as you sleep
In the room of Your Own
In the house that's Your Home.

And the sun rising up
Is the light of Your Eyes

And Your Heart is a bed
For the YOU that will grow

All the days of Your Life

In the air that you breathe

On the ground where you stand

In a place of Your Own

In the world

That's Your Home.